Seven Clues

SEVEN CLUES

by

Kathy Stinson

James Lorimer & Company Ltd., Publishers
Toronto

James Lorimer & Company Ltd. acknowledges the support of the Ontario Arts Council. We acknowledge the support of the Government of Canada through the Book Publishing Industry Development Program (BPIDP) for our publishing activities. We acknowledge the support of the Canada Council for the Arts for our publishing program. We acknowledge the support of the Government of Ontario through the Ontario Media Development Corporation's Ontario Book Initiative.

Cover design: Iris Glaser

The Canada Council | Le Conseil des Arts
for the Arts | du Canada

ONTARIO ARTS COUNCIL
CONSEIL DES ARTS DE L'ONTARIO

Library and Archives of Canada Cataloguing in Publication

Stinson, Kathy
[Seven clues in Pebble Creek]
    Seven clues / Kathy Stinson.
(Streetlights)
First published under title: Seven clues in Pebble Creek.
ISBN-13: 978-1-55028-889-6
ISBN-10: 1-55028-889-X
    I. Title. II. Series.
PS8587.T56S4 2005   jC813'.54   C2005-904861-1

James Lorimer & Company Ltd.,
Publishers
317 Adelaide Street West
Suite 1002
Toronto, Ontario, M5V 1P9
www.lorimer.ca
Printed and bound in Canada.

Distributed in the
United States by:
Orca Book Publishers
P.O. Box 468
Custer, WA USA
98240-0468

Thanks to my editor, Hadley Dyer, for her enthusiasm for this project, for her guidance, and her friendship.

To Peter for the mystery and adventure he brings to my summers

1

IT WAS ONLY a few days into the summer holidays and already Matt was bored. Slouched against the front porch railing, he socked his baseball into his mitt. Sure, he might get to go to camp for the last two weeks of the summer, but so what? That was forever away. In the meantime, he was bored with television reruns. Bored with the same dull games on the slow, old computer his parents said they couldn't afford to replace. Bored with the sound of the baseball slapping into his glove again and again. So bored he was even thinking about cleaning his room, just for something to do.

Matt sighed. He chucked his ball and mitt into the corner of the porch. From the brown grass in front of his house, he picked up his battered bike. In a series of moves that was almost like one move, he slapped his helmet on his head, straightened the crooked seat, and hopped on the bike before the seat could slip out of place again.

On the lawn of the empty house next door stood a "Sold" sign. Matt had spent hours there on Sam's computer — in dungeons and haunted forests. In mazes and at race tracks. But now Sam had moved away. And everybody else was gone somewhere on holidays. Even Matt's best friend, Mike Lennox.

Turning onto the paved path that ran through the shady ravine to Bricker Street, Matt heard a horrible grinding sound. "Not again," he grumbled. He stopped, hooked his drooping bike chain back where it belonged, and headed into the ravine.

Soon he turned onto a narrow dirt path. Over a bumpy section, his bike rattled. Then the path took a sudden dip down and back up again. At the top of the dip, Matt steered sharply right. The path became very narrow. Ferns and weeds caught at his feet. Just short of a boulder that was barely visible among the dense undergrowth, he braked, then let his bike fall into the bushes. He pushed through them and slid down the curved bank to the side of the creek.

This was Matt's favourite spot. Nobody knew about it but him. He came here whenever he had some thinking to do, or when he just wanted to be alone.

Matt wriggled his body into the cool sand of the bank, forming a comfortable hollow there. Splashes of sunlight sparkled on the water. He picked up a pebble from the side of the creek and hurled it. He counted how many times it skipped across the water. Six. He picked up a flatter stone and tried again. Four.

Sam was lucky moving into the city. There was nothing to do in a small town like Pebble Creek. Matt pitched another stone. It glubbed to the bottom of the creek after one skip. He sighed. It was no fun being alone when you had to be.

He climbed back up the riverbank, dragged his bike from the bushes, and started back out of the ravine. Close to the main path, he stopped suddenly and ducked behind the bushes. Shuffling along the paved path was someone he did not want to run into, no matter how bored and lonely he was. Mr. Grubb.

Mr. Grubb was a giant of a man who lived alone in the dark, old house at the end of Booth Street. He was so big that the trousers bagging around his skinny legs stopped far above his sagging socks. The sleeves of his sweater, which he wore no matter what the weather, came nowhere near his wrists. His jowly cheeks pulled his mouth down in a permanent frown.

His trousers, his socks, his slippers, and his sweater were all grey. His hair — shaggy and tucked behind his large ears — was grey, too. So were his piercing eyes and his bushy eyebrows. Everything about the old man seemed to be faded — the bony hand that clutched his wooden cane, and even the sound of his raspy voice. Mr. Grubb was so grey, Matt sometimes wondered if he might be a ghost.

Matt pulled himself more tightly into the bushes. He didn't actually believe in ghosts. Not really. But strange things sometimes happened at the house at the end of Booth Street. Some people said it was haunted.

When Matt was sure Mr. Grubb was well gone, Matt ventured out of the bushes. He turned along the path toward Bricker Street. Outside the variety store, he parked his bike in the bike rack. As he pushed open the screen door, a bell jingled.

"Hi, Matt," greeted the teenager behind the counter. Martha was the only girl Matt had ever met that didn't seem like a member of some alien species. "What'll it be today?" she asked. "Milk? Newspaper for your mom? Gummi eyeballs?"

"Gummi eyeballs are boring," Matt said. "I just came in to say hi."

Martha nudged her wire-framed glasses back up onto the bridge of her nose. "Matt Randall, you love gummi eyeballs. What's wrong?"

"There's nobody around," complained Matt. "Lennox has gone to his cousin's. Abeed and Ven are camping with their dad. There's nothing to do when there's nobody to do it with." Matt flipped through the rack of comics. There was nothing there that he hadn't already read at least six times. He sighed and dragged his feet back to the door.

"Don't look so glum, chum," Martha chirped. "Something will turn up, you'll see."

"Yeah, sure." The bell jingled as he left.

Matt pulled into the driveway just as Nazneen started up his front walk with her bag of mail. "Matt Randall?" she said.

Matt looked up in surprise. "That's me."

"Postcard."

"For me?"

"If you're Matt Randall of number three Booth Street."

"Yeah, I am."

Matt looked at the postcard. Maybe one of his vacationing friends had thought to drop him a line. The postcard said ...

There's something you should look for.
It will bring you great pleasure.
Not coins in a pirate's chest,
But a different sort of treasure.
Be clever, be brave & you'll get to the end.
Along the way, you might need a friend.
The treasure's got old parts,
But new ones, too.
Go to the right bus stop now.
You'll find another clue.

There was no signature.

Matt stared at the message. *Go to the right bus stop. A different sort of treasure.* Why had the postcard been sent to him? Was this some kind of treasure hunt?

Nazneen dropped the rest of the mail into the Randalls' mailbox. As she passed Matt again, she winked, then continued on her route, whistling.

Again Matt examined the postcard. On the front was a picture of a girl beside a windmill. She was wearing wooden shoes and holding tulips.

Did the postcard come from Holland?

It couldn't have. It didn't have a foreign postage stamp. Studying the faint postmark, Matt barely made out the word *Mazurk*. The name of a town not far from Pebble Creek.

Could someone have bought the postcard in Holland and not sent it until they got home to Mazurk? Maybe, but Matt didn't think he knew anyone one who had ever been to Holland, or who lived in Mazurk.

"Mom," he called, going inside. "Mom, do we know anybody ...?"

She had the phone tucked between her ear and her shoulder. Bills and bank statements were spread out on the table in front of her. Crossly, she waved Matt away.

Matt shrugged. Rereading the message, he wandered back inside.

You might need a friend, the card said. Terrific. Where was he supposed to find a friend when everyone was away? Matt looked longingly at the houses across the street. He looked between them to the empty baseball field. There was no one around for baseball or a treasure hunt.

But so what? he decided. The note just said he *might* need a friend. It also said that at the right bus stop he would find another clue. It wouldn't hurt to look. He jammed the postcard into his pocket and repeated his usual smooth helmet-and-bike-seat routine.

A few minutes later his bike clattered to the ground beside the Bricker Variety store. He pushed open the screen door.

"Martha, what do you think about …?"

But Martha was not alone. Leaning on the counter across from her was a tall girl with pink hair and green lips. She had jagged yellow lines painted around her eyes. It was obvious that she was into Pebble Creek's weird hair-styling place big time. It was called The Purple Flamingo after one of the strange hairdos they did there — mostly for teenagers, but some adults went in for that stuff, too. Matt's friend Lennox thought the colourful people who came out of The Purple

Flamingo were funny. Matt was embarrassed to admit that he found them a bit scary.

"You again?" asked Martha. " What's new?"

The other girl stared down at him.

"Just …" He couldn't ask Martha about the postcard now. "Nothing."

"Oh, Martha," drawled her friend, "he's cute."

Feeling about two inches tall, Matt darted for the door. He let it slam behind him. He was leaning against the side of the building, feeling stupid, when he spotted something unusual.

Quite low on the bus stop in front of Bricker Variety was a piece of paper. Maybe it was a scrap that had been blown against the post by the wind.

Matt stepped a bit closer. The paper had been folded and tacked to the post. *It must be a clue.* Matt pulled it free. He tucked it into his pocket and grabbed his bike.

The paper made a comfortable lump in his pocket. He turned onto the path leading to his place by the river. Bump … rattle, rattle … dip down, dip up … sharp turn right. Narrow, even narrower ... to the boulder. Through the bushes and down the bank.

So what if he couldn't figure out who was behind the strange clue, or what it was he might be looking for, or why he might need a friend to help find it? He had found the second clue, and the clues were going to lead him to treasure.

His hands shaking, Matt pulled the lump of paper from his pocket and unfolded it.

2

THE PAPER WAS blank. Blank on both sides. Matt looked at his postcard again. *Be clever*, it said.

He should have known that would count him out. Brains had never been his strong point. And if he was too stupid to find even one clue, how did he think he could ever find a treasure? With the heel of his shoe, Matt dug a hole in the sand. Into the hole he dropped the blank paper, and buried it. He climbed back up the bank.

Riding around town, Matt wished he had never seen the mysterious postcard. Now he felt bored, lonely — and stupid.

Passing the gas station, he noticed another bus stop with another piece of paper tacked to it. He rode on past. Was this someone's idea of a joke? Well, he wouldn't let them make *him* look like some kind of fool.

But what if there really was another clue? Was it stupid to go on looking? Or stupid to give up on finding it so quickly?

Wheeling down the street, Matt saw that a scrap of paper was tacked to the bus stop by the library, too. A group of teenagers lay in the grass nearby. Pedalling slowly, Matt wished Lennox was with him. He'd know what to do.

Matt circled back to the library's bus stop. It wouldn't hurt just to check. He yanked the paper free and tucked it into his pocket. When he straightened the seat on his bike and pulled away, a wave of laughter spread through the gang on the grass. Matt felt his face go red.

So, it *was* a joke. So much for his hopes of some kind of cool summer mystery to solve. Pedalling fast along Bricker Street, he told himself it didn't matter. He hadn't really believed in the treasure hunt anyway. If he hadn't been so bored, he wouldn't have paid any attention at all to the stupid postcard. So, he was just back to being bored old Matt Randall looking forward to a boring summer. So what.

Matt pulled up beside a recycling bin in front of the post office. He unfolded the useless scrap of paper, ready to throw it out along with the first scrap he'd found. Just before dropping them into basket, he noticed some printing on the new one. It was just like the scrunched-up printing on the postcard. His heart pounding, Matt sat down on the curb.

Nazneen trudged up beside him with her empty mailbag. "How's the detective business?" she asked.

Matt shrugged. Nazneen winked. When she had gone inside, Matt read:

To find the next clue, you must go
Where books are lined up row on row.
Six shelves in on the right-hand side

Look in the back of a book very wide.
Be sure no one sees you near this spot
And with these clues do not get caught.

A shiver tickled up Matt's spine. But he knew what he had to do. Back to the library he beetled.

Glad to see that the teenagers on the grass were gone, he strode up the broad steps and into the old, stone building. In the cool, quiet room, several people were lined up to surf the Internet. A few others were thumbing through magazines. The children's librarian was helping a father choose some books for his daughter.

Matt headed down the right-hand side of the library, counting shelves till he reached the sixth. Feeling very out of place in the adult section, he gave a hurried look for a book that was *very wide*. They were all wider than anything he'd ever read.

He pulled out a book that looked especially thick — a blue one. Inside its back cover he found nothing. He checked a few other big books, but no luck.

Then, Matt saw a thick, grey book high above him. It was definitely thicker than any other book on the shelf. It had to be the one.

He pulled over a nearby footstool to stand on, but even at a full stretch he couldn't reach it. *This must be where the friend comes in,* he thought.

As Matt stepped down from the stool, he was frozen in his tracks by a movement behind the books. Someone was looking at the books on the other side of the shelf.

No, not at the books, Matt realized. Someone was looking at him. A pair of eyes with jagged yellow lines painted around them! *Be sure no one sees you near this spot.*

In a gruff whisper, the green lips behind the books said, "Find what you're after?"

Matt bolted. He scrambled down the steps of the library, grabbed his bike, and pedalled hard through the ravine. Sweat trickled down his face and soaked the back of his shirt. He steered his bike along one of the side paths that led to a wooden bridge over the creek.

Panting, he dropped his bike on the bridge, plunked himself down on the wooden planks, and yanked off his sneakers and socks. As he dangled his feet in the cool water, his racing heart began to beat more normally. How was it that Martha's crazy friend could make him feel like such a loser?

Matt jumped when the boards *thump-bump*ed behind him. Approaching on a brand new, hyper-grind, freestyle BMX was David Varvarikos.

Matt stared for a moment. Could this really be David? He didn't think he'd ever seen him on a bike before. At school, when David's work was done, which was almost always, the guy never goofed off or shot spitballs. He stayed at his desk, reading. Even at recess he stood by the wall of the school with his nose in a book. He walked home that way, too. And David never played sports. Unless you counted skipping games with the girls, which Matt most definitely did not. The one time Ms. Symon had made David play baseball in gym class, he didn't even know how to hold the bat.

David dismounted, leaned his bike against the bridge railing, and sat down. Matt tried not to look at the fabulous set of wheels. He tried not to look at the geek sitting beside him with his arms looped through the rails.

"That your bike?" Matt finally asked. Its tires were jet black. Its red paint and chrome handlebars shone.

"Yup."

"Looks brand new."

"Yup."

"I didn't think you knew how to ride a bike."

"I know how. I just never had one of my own before."

Oh, great. David was already a bit hard to take. With this bike, he would be a royal pain for sure.

David said, "My parents gave it to me for passing with honours."

"You're kidding." Matt laughed. "Bet you couldn't *not* pass with honours if you tried."

"I know. It's still a good excuse for a present."

"I'll have to try that one on my parents. A present for passing." Matt turned the idea over in his mind. "I wonder if I could talk them into buying a new computer. Ours is so slow you can't play anything faster than Solitaire on it, and surfing the Net's just hopeless."

David practically choked. "I doubt it! A halfway decent computer costs way more than a new bike, which you obviously need and it seems they can't afford to buy you."

David pulled a paperback book from the waistband of his shorts and started to read. His straight, black hair hung neatly. His white shirt was tucked neatly into his crisply ironed shorts. His nose was neatly buried in his book. Matt felt like dumping neat David into the river.

But that would be too obvious. He had a much better idea.

3

"WANNA RACE?" Matt challenged David.

"Okay."

David continued to read while Matt pulled his feet out of the water and dried them with his socks, which he then tied to his handlebars. He shoved his feet into his tattered sneakers and stood with his old, blue bike. "You coming?"

"Okay." David looked up. "I was just waiting for you." He tucked his book into the back of his waistband and pulled up his socks.

"Ready?" Matt tossed on his helmet and set off in the direction of the quarry.

David mounted his bike and followed. "Ready."

I bet you're not ready, Matt thought, *for what I've got in mind.*

The wheels of Matt's plain, old bike and David's new BMX spun freely along the pavement. The breeze cooled the boys' faces and necks. But they had not gone far when Matt's bicycle ground to a stop. "Oh, not now," he groaned.

As he kneeled to reattach the chain, David crowed, "I'd better lead." And he flashed past Matt in a blur of red.

"That little …!" Matt put on a burst of speed to catch up. Above the north wall of the quarry he slowed down just enough to casually pedal past David.

"Hey!"

Before David could pass him again, Matt veered left, his tires thunking off the main path to a dirt path below. *We'll see how smart you are now,* he thought.

Matt led David on a meandering route among clumps of clay and rock to the quarry floor below. He bumped over large stones and made sudden turns at odd angles to avoid holes and clumps of boulder. Where he was leading David wasn't really a path at all, and he expected at any moment to hear David's BMX cracking up behind him.

But soon, with both bicycles still intact, the two boys stood on the quarry floor. Matt shaded his eyes and gazed up the steep walls at the zigzagging route they had taken down. He huffed to catch his breath. "I guess you're good at more than just reading," he said.

David beamed. "Did I surprise you?"

"Yeah."

David might be a pain, but he could sure ride a mean bike. There were a couple of spots where Matt had wondered if he'd make it down in one piece. "That was a pretty rough ride," he said.

"Are you kidding?" David answered. "It was nothing."

"Oh, you think so?" Beside the route the boys had just taken was a sheer cliff of smooth sand. "Then I guess you could ride down there easy, too, eh?"

David looked up where Matt was pointing. He gripped his handlebar tightly. "Sure."

"Okay, then. Let's go."

Together the boys dragged their bikes back up through the rocks and bushes, and over to the top of the wall of sand.

"Okay?" said David.

"On the count of three," dared Matt.

Together they counted. "One. Two. Three."

David started down the steep slope. The front wheel of his bike sank quickly into the soft sand. From the top of the cliff, Matt watched as the bike suddenly stopped and over its shining handlebar, David flipped.

As David rolled down the slope, his arms kept reaching out, and reaching out again, but there was nothing for his hands to grasp hold of, and he just kept on rolling.

"David!" Matt yelled, sliding down the sand on his back. He couldn't believe *anyone* would actually try riding down the cliff. For sure Lennox would never fall for a crazy dare like that.

When David finally stopped tumbling, his body lay still on the floor of the quarry far below.

"I'm coming, David," Matt croaked. It was hard to hurry when he had to keep leaning back to stop himself from pitching forward down the sand, too.

When Matt finally reached the bottom of the cliff, he saw that David's clothes were all twisted around his body. His helmet had come off and his hair was full of sand and sticking to his sweaty face. His cheeks were flushed. But at least he was breathing. Matt could see his chest rising and falling with each breath.

David groaned. He opened his eyes and quickly closed them again. Matt shielded David's face from the bright sun. Slowly, David managed to sit up.

"David, I thought you were supposed to be smart."

David shook the sand out of his shirt and tucked it back into his shorts. "Oh no, my book," he fretted. "I lost my book."

"Forget the book! You could have killed yourself! What were you trying to prove?"

David watched a handful of sand sift through his fingers. "I know what everybody says about me, you know. You think because I don't say much at school, and go to Greek school on Saturdays, that I'm just a wimp."

Matt emptied sand out of one of his shoes.

"I thought if I didn't ride down with you after we counted to three, that you'd keep thinking it."

"So, you'd rather I thought you were an idiot?"

David shrugged.

Matt wandered to a pile of rocks near where David had landed. He picked one up and hurled it at the "No Dumping" sign. It clanged when it hit. Matt reached for another rock. *Clang.*

On his feet, David started pitching rocks at the target, too.

"Guess you're okay, eh?" Matt said.

David hurled another rock and missed. *Thud.* "I'm okay."

Matt looked at him for a few moments, then took a deep breath. "Listen," he said. "There's this … well, there's this book I have to get at the library, and I could kind of use … like … a hand."

"What's it called? Maybe I have it." *Clang*.

"It's grey and really fat. I forget what it's called."

"You want to get a book, but you don't even know the title?"

"It's not the book I want, exactly." Why did David have to ask so many dumb questions?

"Then what *do* you want?"

Hesitantly, Matt explained. "Okay, so there's this paper that … um … my mom thinks she left in this book …" *Thud*. "Only I don't think I can reach it."

"So, why doesn't your mom get it herself?"

"Listen, David, I just need you to give me a boost so I can get this paper out of this book. Will you do that or not?"

"Okay!" David snapped. "I'll help you get your stupid paper."

"Now?"

"Whatever you say, *boss*!" Sarcasm dripped from David's voice.

Without another word, the boys fetched their bikes. They rode out of the quarry and through the streets without speaking.

On the stairs of the library, Matt said, "I have to tell you a couple of things before we go in."

"What?"

"Well, for one thing, we've got to make sure nobody sees us."

"Why?"

"We just do. And, don't wander around. Just follow me in, then out. Okay?"

"I guess so," David said. "But I'd sure like to know who put you in charge."

"Look," Matt argued, "it's my clue, isn't it?"

As soon as the words were out of his mouth, he realized his mistake.

4

"CLUE?" PRESSED DAVID. "What clue?"

Matt kicked a pebble down the library steps to the road. How could he get David to help now, without giving away everything?

"And don't cook up any more of that story about a note your mother left in a book," David warned. "I'm not helping you till you tell me the truth."

Slowly Matt walked down the steps of the library. He sat under a maple tree and reluctantly pulled the postcard and the crumpled bus-stop clue from his pocket. Just then, Martha walked by. "Hey, Martha," called Matt. "I thought you were working."

"Someone's covering for me so I could get this

book of poetry back to the library. It's way overdue."

"You read poetry?" asked David. "Me, too."

"Martha!" said a husky voice. Down the steps of the library pranced Martha's friend from The Purple Flamingo. The plainer girl's brown pony-tail swung from side to side as she ran to meet her. How was it, Matt wondered, that Martha and this pink-haired weirdo had started hanging around together?

David took the postcard from Matt and read it. "So, do you know who sent this?"

"No."

"But you're actually doing what it says?"

"Why not? It says there's a treasure, and there can't be anything dangerous about it if all the clues are out in the open."

David flicked the postcard onto the grass. "Can't you tell when someone's pulling your leg?"

Matt blushed. "But there was another clue at the bus stop. What about that?"

"What about it?" David scoffed. "I still say there's no treasure."

"Yeah, well, you don't know everything." Matt grabbed up the postcard and stuffed it in his jeans pocket. "And what do you care if there's any treasure or not? I only asked you to help me get the book down. I didn't ask you to do the whole thing with me."

"Wait a second," David said. "All this *be sure no one sees you* and *don't get caught* stuff? This could be dangerous! If I'm going to help you with anything, then I'm in on the treasure, too."

"*You* wait a second!" Matt stood up and glared down at David. "One minute you're saying there's no treasure. The next minute, you're claiming your share!" He stomped off to get his bike from the rack. "Just forget it, okay? I'll find someone else to get the book for me."

"Hey, wait, Matt! I'll do it!"

Matt gripped the handlebar of his scruffy bike.

"If you let me help," David pleaded, "I'll let you ride my BMX."

Matt paused. The seat of his own bike hung crookedly by a rusty piece of metal. Several spokes were missing from the back wheel. In the rack beside Matt's bike shone the gleaming hyper-grind, freestyle BMX, with its black, padded handgrips, seat cover to match, and red-rimmed mag wheels.

Matt pretended to think over David's offer, but really there was no one else to help him. And for a chance to ride on David's bike …?

"Okay. Tomorrow, then."

The reading area in the library was full of people and, as usual, there was a lineup for the computer terminals. But it seemed nobody even noticed the boys striding into the adult section as if they belonged there.

What if someone else had taken out the grey book on the sixth shelf? What if that creepy teenager with the pink hair had it? Matt checked that there was no one browsing, or pretending to browse, on the other side of his shelf, then looked up where he hoped the book would be.

It was still there. Matt got David to make a

cradle with his hands, placed one foot into it, and reached up.

"Ouch!" David yelped. "My fingers!"

He let go, and Matt landed on the floor with a thud. "Ow!"

Suddenly the library was very quiet. Matt felt everyone looking in their direction. Fortunately, he had managed to grab hold of the book just before David dropped him. He shook it quickly, a paper slipped out, and Matt shoved the book onto a lower shelf. When he picked himself up, he found himself face-to-armpit with the librarian.

"What," she asked sternly, "are you boys doing in this section of the library? Don't you know the children's books are over there?" She pointed like the Scarecrow in *The Wizard of Oz*.

Matt could only swallow in reply, but David spoke up. "I had to get a note that my mom left in the back of a book she had out," said David.

"And did you find it?"

"Yes. Thank you."

"Then I think," the librarian said, "that you

should be taking it home to her, don't you?"

"Yes, ma'am," David said. "That's what we were just about to do."

Under the tree in front of the library, Matt and David collapsed on the ground in a fit of laughter. Matt mimicked David's, "'Yes, ma'am. That's what we were just about to do.'"

David hugged his sides, laughing.

Matt grinned. "And what was that about a note your mother left in a library book?"

"It came in handy, that dumb story."

Matt jumped on David's stomach and pretended he was punching him out.

Still laughing, David flipped Matt off him and onto his back in the grass. "So, let's see that note."

"Not so fast, David. First, you owe me a ride on your bike."

Riding into the wooded ravine, Matt thrilled to the feel of the spanking-new BMX beneath him.

Cycling alongside him, David said, "You know what? I think I know who sent the postcard."

"Who?"

"A Dutch poet," said David. "A really bad Dutch poet."

"Since when do I know a Dutch poet?"

"Since for ages. I know her, too."

Matt looked at David blankly. "Okay, so, who is it?"

David laughed. "It's obvious, really."

Matt braked to a sudden stop. "Would you quit with the high-and-mighty act? It's not like I don't know you're a brainer already. Just tell me — who is it?"

"If I do," David bargained, "then I want in on the rest of the treasure hunt."

"No way." Matt dropped David's bike to the ground.

"Easy! That's a valuable vehicle!"

"*So-orry,*" Matt said sarcastically. He grabbed his bike from David, straightened its seat, and pedalled away.

"Hey!" David called. "Don't you want to know who the mystery poet is?"

Matt paused, then rode away furiously. He didn't stop till he got to the wooden bridge.

As he stared down at the water gurgling over the coloured pebbles on the bottom of the creek, David pulled up beside him.

Matt mumbled, "Okay. Who?"

"And I do the treasure hunt with you?" David pressed.

"Yeah, yeah."

"Scout's honour?"

"Scout's honour."

"Cross your heart?"

"Cross my heart."

"Spit on a rock?"

Matt groaned. "David, just tell me who sent the postcard before I change my mind."

5

"The mystery poet," David announced, "is Martha."

"She's Dutch?"

"What kind of name do you think Van Loon is? Pig Latin?"

"But if it's Martha, it can't be a *real* treasure hunt," Matt objected. "If it's Martha, it's just some stupid game."

"So? Even if it is, it's not like we have anything better to do."

Matt shrugged. With the toe of his shoe, he knocked a stone off the bridge into the water. If Martha *was* responsible for the clues, did that mean her weird friend might be involved, too? Is that why she was at the library the day before? Hoping not, he pulled the third clue from his pocket.

Together the boys read:

Rocks, not paper, are found in a quarry,
Except for today, and your only worry
Is under which rocks will you look?
By the north wall? Or by the brook?
The treasure has big parts, little parts, too.
It's okay for one, even better for two.

"Not the quarry," groaned Matt. "It's so hot down there."

"We could go get an ice cream first."

Inside the Pebble Creek Ice Cream store, David held a place in the long line while Matt hung around the Space Demons video game in the corner. The spaceship demolished the last of the demons, and the tall girl playing the game walked away laughing. Matt stepped forward and dropped his quarter into the slot, ready for action. He'd played for only a minute when the space demons destroyed his ship. A beefy teenager elbowed Matt out of his away.

Under his breath, Matt cursed.

"What did you say?"

"Nothing." Matt joined David in line.

Afterward, on the bench in front of the store, Matt licked a chocolatey drip running down the side of his cone. "I'm trying to eat my way through all the flavours of ice cream before the end of the summer," he said.

"Me too," said David. "How many have you had so far?"

"How many have you?"

"I asked you first."

"Five, I think."

"Oh," said David. "I've just had three."

"Yeah, me, too," Matt admitted.

"Turkey." David laughed.

Matt grinned. "You know what would be a good treasure?"

"What?"

"Gift certificates for a whole summer's worth of ice cream cones."

David crunched into the edge of his cone. "I think it will be something even better than that."

"Like what?"

"Maybe a tremendous pile of money."

"I heard of a guy once, who found a suitcase full of money in a ditch. He turned it over to the police, and when nobody claimed it, he got to keep it." Matt looked over the clue again. "But what we're looking for isn't money."

"How do you know?"

"Money's small, for one thing. But the note says big parts and little parts."

"Could be big bills like hundreds and little bills like fives."

"The note also says the treasure would be better for two. Who wants to share money?"

"You're right about that," agreed David. He nudged Matt and nodded toward someone across the street.

Walking out of The Purple Flamingo hair

salon was a girl whose hair was dyed in strips of purple, red, orange, yellow, green, and blue. It looked like a rainbow running down her head. Rainbow stripes also swirled across her skin-tight tank top. Fluorescent green pants hugged her legs. On her feet she wore neon pink runners.

Matt shook his head as ice cream melted down his wrist.

The rainbow girl's boyfriend looked pretty strange, too. Long spikes of black hair grew grew up the middle of his shaved scalp. He, too, wore neon pink runners — with blue jeans and a white T-shirt.

"Why do they do that?" muttered Matt.

"Beats me," David said. "But I heard that a pair of twins once came two hundred miles just to get their hair done at The Purple Flamingo."

"Freaky."

As the couple crossed the street, David read the words on the spiky-haired guy's T-shirt. *Have you hugged a tree today?* Close up, the boys could see that the rainbow-haired girl had a grey cloud painted across her forehead and over one eye. Brilliant blue raindrops rained down her cheeks.

"Freaky," said David.

"Freaky," repeated Matt.

"Heavy."

"Maximum weird."

"Groovy."

Matt laughed. "You're crazy."

"You're crazy," echoed David. "Let's go find the next clue."

"Race you to the quarry."

Matt and David sped up Stony Road. Matt was in the lead as they skidded around the corner onto Bricker Street. A dump truck clunked up the road out of the quarry. Into the hot cloud of dust it left behind, the boys rode.

When the dust had settled, Matt dropped his bike and shaded his eyes against the bright sun. He took a broad look around the hot quarry and said, "There's hundreds of rocks here."

"Thousands," moaned David.

Except for the strip of sand down the middle

of the quarry, there were rocks — jagged ones and smooth ones, large ones and small ones — scattered and heaped everywhere.

"Maybe," Matt whimpered, "it's more like millions. We'll *never* find the next clue."

"Yes, we will," David reached down and picked up a small rock. "It will just take patience."

"For you, maybe," Matt said. "Not for me."

"What do you mean?"

"No way am I spending all day down here turning over a billion rocks." Matt moved toward his bike. "What if there isn't even another clue?"

"Of course there's another clue," David argued. "Why wouldn't there be?"

"Nobody's going to make me look like a fool over some stupid, fake treasure. I say forget it."

"Sure, go ahead and forget it," David yelled. "But when I get through all this …?" He took in the quarry with a sweep of his arm. "… and when I've found the treasure? You can just forget that, too!"

Matt mounted his bike and started riding away. "You won't find it."

"Yes, I will," David insisted. "And if you quit now, it's all mine. And who will look like a fool then, Matt?"

Matt looked back through the dust being kicked up by the spinning wheels of his bike. David was already bent over and turning rocks over one by one. As Matt pedalled through the quarry toward the exit, heat brushed his face. *Who will look like a fool then?*

Again Matt glanced over his shoulder. He couldn't go back there, to where David was throwing rocks to one side, or it would look as if he cared what David said. But he couldn't just let David find the clue either.

At the side of the road, under a thick layer of dust, sat an old dump truck with a flat tire and a broken windshield. Matt veered off the road to think. Behind the truck there were, of course, more rocks.

He could look here and David wouldn't even know he was looking. He could find the next clue all on his own — why not? — and eventually the treasure, too. Without David.

Matt leaned his bike against the side of the truck. Someone had drawn a big X in the dust on its door. *X marks the spot*, Matt thought. Did this X mark the spot where a fourth clue would be found?

The sun beat down hard as Matt pitched aside small rocks and rolled the larger rocks over, watching carefully for a piece of paper the whole time he worked. As he shoved and heaved, his hands became dusty and sore. The muscles in his back began to ache.

What a stupid way to be spending his summer holiday. Maybe he should have just gone to that ceramics class that his mom had wanted to sign him up for. Sure, it would have been lame, but this wasn't?

Wiping sweat from his brow, he left a gritty streak of dirt across his hot face. Matt straightened his sore back and peeked around the truck. David was still turning over rocks, but very slowly now. Sure that X marked the spot where the next clue would be found, Matt shoved aside another rock.

He heard in the distance the cool, rippling sound of the river and licked his parched lips. A dusty envelope lay on the ground at his feet. A long moment passed before it sank into his heat-muddled mind what it meant. He ran his sweating hands through his sandy hair. He picked up the envelope and opened it.

The words printed on the paper inside made no sense, but things Matt read often didn't. And today he was hot. He was tired. He was thirsty. He tucked the fourth clue into his pocket and rode to his secret spot on the other side of the river. He splashed cool water over his face and into his mouth. Then he read the clue again. It was very short.

6

Is a shop where they sell ham and baloney
What you want to know you will find out
And you could spend a pretty penny.
The next clue is waiting for you there.

Still, the message made no sense. But the words *where they sell ham and baloney* could mean only one place.

Matt ambled into Joe's Deli on Stony Road.

Behind the counter Joe was weighing a mound of sliced salami for Mrs. Miffin, while her two-year-old, Lisa, climbed out of her stroller. Matt glanced quickly around, trying to figure where the next clue might be planted.

When he lifted the lid off the pickle barrel, the smell of garlic and vinegar rose from inside. But of course there was nothing in the barrel but pickles.

Matt felt a tug on his shorts.

"Hi, Lisa." He crouched down. "Lisa got a pickle?"

Lisa nodded and stuck the pickle under Matt's nose.

"No, thanks, Lisa," he said. "You eat it."

Lisa stuck out her tongue and showed Matt her mouthful of semi-chewed chunks of green. He groaned and looked away. Under the edge of the counter were stuck several grey and pink lumps of old gum. But no paper.

Matt eyed the boxes on the counter by the cash register, and looked around the cash register itself for a piece of paper that didn't belong.

"Goodbye, Mrs. Miffin," Joe said. He turned to Matt. "You want something, young man?"

Matt pulled a hot pepperoni stick from the box on the counter and paid Joe for it. It wasn't the fifth clue, but it was better than nothing.

Standing in front of the deli, Matt bit the wrapper off his pepperoni. He looked up to see David sailing by on his bike, waving a slip of paper. "Another clue, Matt! Too bad for you!"

Too bad for you, too, David, if your clue is as useless as mine, Matt thought. But why had he and David both found clues in the quarry?

Matt looked again at the clue that had sent them there. He noticed something he hadn't noticed before. It said, *Under which rocks for clues will you look?*

Rocks — as in more than one. Same with *clues.*

Matt pedalled slowly up Stony Road.

Maybe he needed the other piece of paper, too, for the clue to make sense. If he could get a look at David's note somehow, maybe then he could figure out where he was supposed to go to find the next clue.

Matt chewed the spicy meat stick as he rode. He spotted David making a turn, and followed him across the top of the north quarry wall. When David parked his bike on the bridge, so did Matt.

He tried to look apologetic. "Sorry I got mad and didn't help you in the quarry, David."

"I guess *so*," David said. "Especially since I found the next clue."

"Yup." Matt hung his head. "I sure do wish I had your brains."

David looked at his clue. "Well, too bad for you."

Matt glanced quickly at David's paper and caught the words *Stony* and *care*.

"Forget it." David snatched the paper away.

"David," Matt said, "didn't the note at the library say the *clues* in the quarry would be under *rocks*?"

"Yeah. So what?"

"So, did you find both clues?"

David paused for just a second. "Sure."

"Well, then, why aren't you over on Stony Road looking for the *next* clue?"

David pulled up his already pulled-up socks and tucked in his already tucked-in shirt. "Maybe I've already found it."

Matt took the clue he had found by the truck from his pocket. He ran it slowly through his fingers, in front of David's nose. "Oh, really?"

"You sneak," David muttered.

"Trouble is," Matt said, "your clue doesn't make sense, does it? Your half clue, I should say."

David clenched his fist tightly around the paper he had found. "How did you know?"

"Because mine doesn't either," Matt admitted.

"Let me see."

"Not till I see yours."

"How about we trade?"

The boys exchanged slips of paper. Munching on the remains of his pepperoni, Matt read:

Out on the road that is called Stony
That's not the one you care about.
In a place where there are colours many
Go to the part where you feel hot air.

Matt stared at David's paper and read it again. He was no farther ahead than he was before.

But what if David figured out the note *he* was busy reading? He'd be able to get the next clue by himself, and maybe even the treasure, depending how many clues there were in all. Darn! He should never have let David see …

"Even together," David said, "these notes don't make sense."

Matt reluctantly, but with some relief, agreed. "It's all just a jumble of words."

David pounded the bridge railing and looked again at the note in his hand.

"Wait a minute," he said. "Read what you've got there out loud."

Matt read.

"Okay, now listen." David read his slip of paper. "So?"

"Words in yours rhyme with words in mine," David pointed out. "Baloney, Stony, out, about …"

"So what?"

"What if we put the two clues together, one line from mine, then one line from yours? Back and forth."

Put together like that, the new clue said:

Out on the road that is called Stony
Is a shop where they sell ham and baloney.
That's not the one that you care about.
What you want to know you will find out
In a place where there are colours many
And you could spend a pretty penny.
Go to the part where you feel hot air.
The next clue is waiting for you there.

"David, you are brilliant." Matt let out a spicy burp.

David said, "But not brilliant enough to know where we're meant to go for the next clue."

"Think. *Colours*. Spending a lot of money."

"*Hot air*," David added.

Matt drummed his fingers on the railing. "I know! The hair dryer at The Purple Flamingo!"

"Hey," laughed David, "you're not nearly as stupid as I thought."

"Gee, thanks. But there's still one problem.

We can't just walk into The Purple Flamingo and check out the hair dryer."

"So, you go in and get your hair done, and check the dryer then," David suggested.

"No way." Matt shook his head. "*You* go in and get *your* hair done."

"Are you kidding?" David said. "My mom would kill me."

"And you think mine won't?"

"Not like mine would, I bet you anything. You don't know how strict my parents are."

Matt thought about how David always kept his clothes so neat, and how hard he worked at school. Maybe he could guess how they'd feel about a hairdo from The Purple Flamingo.

"How about this, then?" Matt said. "I'll sacrifice my head to get near that hair dryer, if you'll sacrifice the bucks I'll need to do it."

David smiled. "How about I pay two-thirds and you pay one-third?"

"Come on, David. It's more than two-thirds of my head that stands to come out looking pretty weird in all this."

"Okay, okay. I'll get my money."

Near the end of the path at the edge of the woods, David suddenly stopped. "Look."

Across the Booth Street cul-de-sac, standing on the sidewalk and talking together, were Matt's mother and Mr. Grubb.

"That guy gives me the creeps," said David.

"Me, too," agreed Matt. "There's always this bizarre stuff in his garbage. Like one day there was a pair of lady's legs."

"I saw those, too." David shuddered.

"And what about all the strange boxes that he gets delivered?"

Matt's mother looked at Mr. Grubb and shrugged. What could they be talking about?

"I heard that he buries people in his garden," David said.

"What?"

"You know that book about the old ladies who hire companions, and then poison them and bury them in their garden?"

"No."

"I forgot," David said. "You wouldn't have read it."

"Well, what about it?"

"That's what Mr. Grubb does."

"How do you know?"

"I live right next door to him, remember?"

"Cree-eepy."

"You're not kidding. The smells that sometimes come out of that place ..."

Matt grimaced.

Just then Mr. Grubb turned his sagging face in their direction. The bristles of hair in his bushy eyebrows jerked up and down, as if he was surprised to see the boys, and his eyes opened wide.

David turned and pedalled furiously into the wooded ravine. And Matt followed.

7

THE BOYS STOOD outside The Purple Flamingo, waiting for it to open. David tried to pat Matt's sandy-brown mop of curls. Matt waved him off.

"May I suggest for you," David teased, "the Pink Puff? Or perhaps the Halo of Many Coloured Spikes would suit you."

When the door clicked unlocked, Matt stood to go in.

"Good luck," David said.

Inside the hair salon, strange smells tickled Matt's nose. Behind the counter, the shop owner — with rainbow hair and clouds and raindrops on her face — filed her blue fingernails. Matt looked at the list of hairstyles and prices on the board, and decided she must have what was called the "Summer Storm."

Summer Storm shouted above the din of the music blasting from the radio, "You want something?"

For the amount of money Matt had in his pocket, he had two choices. The Bald Eagle hairdo or the Purple Flamingo.

"What's the Bald Eagle?" Matt asked.

The hairdresser wrapped her fingers around Matt's head just above his ears. "Everything from here up, we shave off. Then we rub in a product to keep your hair from growing too fast and bake it under the dryer. You know, so you can keep the Bald Eagle look for a while."

Matt gulped. He'd been hoping for something less drastic. "What about the Purple Flamingo?"

"We style the hair on top of your head in the shape of a flamingo's neck and head, and set it with a purple gel." With her hands, the girl indicated the sides of Matt's head, where they would then shape the flamingo's body. "We usually have to use rollers for that part," she said, "but with your thick hair, we could just fluff up the hair as we work in the gel."

Matt tried not to grimace. "Would I go under the hair dryer for that one?"

"Just on the no-blow setting, to help set the shape."

Matt swallowed. "Okay."

"You sure? Some people don't like the Purple Flamingo very much because it only lasts till the next time you wash your hair."

"Fine," Matt said. "That's just … fine."

Summer Storm pointed toward the back of the shop. "Go behind that wall to the left and we'll wash your hair." She went back to filing her blue fingernails.

Anxious to get on with the treasure hunt, but not anxious for how he was going to end up looking, Matt walked stiffly toward the back. At the wall on his left, he turned.

Beside the sink a tall girl smiled a green smile. "You're that cute little friend of Martha's, aren't you?" she said in her husky voice. "Matt, right? My name is Rapture. Oh, just look at the beautiful thick hair you have!"

Was she being sarcastic, or what? With girls, who could ever tell? But this time he wasn't going to bolt. Matt slumped into the chair.

Rapture tied a plastic apron around his neck, tipped him back, and turned on the tap. Jets of warm water blasted his head. "Let me know if it gets too hot," Rapture said, and began massaging shampoo through Matt's hair.

Her long nails stabbed and jabbed his scalp. The hard edge of the basin dug into the back of his neck. As Rapture rinsed the shampoo from his hair, she hummed along with the music that blared from the speakers overhead.

Suddenly the water went freezing cold. Matt sprang upright and the icy water trickled down the back of his shirt.

"That's good for your scalp," Rapture laughed. She tipped Matt back over the sink and squeezed the water from his hair.

Man, was she trying to wring the hair right out of his head, or what?

With a neon yellow towel, Rapture rubbed Matt's head so vigorously his scalp tingled. Finally she declared him ready for his Flamingo. Matt glanced in the mirror — yes, he still had his hair — and moved to the next chair.

Right away, Summer Storm started yanking a comb through his wet curls. He winced with each snag and tangle. Hadn't these people ever heard of conditioner? Matt smiled faintly at David, standing outside with his nose to the window.

"That your friend out there?" Summer Storm asked.

"Sort of."

"Is he going to get done, too?"

"No."

"Too bad. With that straight black hair of his, we could give him a great Night Sky."

"Yup, too bad." Whatever a Night Sky hairdo might look like.

Summer Storm set down her comb. A cold

glop of goo plopped on the top of Matt's head. Soon a flamingo's head began to take shape, and Matt began to wish he and David had never figured out that fourth clue. *How many more clues would there be, anyway?* he wondered.

With her fingers and purple gel and the point of her comb, Summer Storm fluffed flamingo "feathers" all around Matt's head. "Just a little trim now," the stylist said, "and you're ready for the dryer."

The cold razor buzzed and nipped the back of his neck. Matt looked in the mirror at the stupid-looking kid with the stupid-looking purple flamingo sitting on his head. He wished it wasn't him.

When Matt stood to go to the dryer, David held up the slips of paper from the quarry.

Matt shot him a scathing look. Did David really think Matt had forgotten why he was here? Did he think Matt was having a good time?

As Summer Storm led Matt to the hair dryer, he felt like a guy in some movie, heading for the electric chair. Before sitting down, he quickly inspected the outside of the dryer. The next clue wasn't there. *That's okay*, Matt told himself as he sat down. There were other parts of the dryer where it could be.

Summer Storm flipped a couple of switches and lowered the dome over his head. Matt raised his eyes to check the inside rim.

There was nothing there.

He checked the floor around the chair in case the clue had fallen or blown out. Nothing. He lifted the dryer off his head so he could check further up inside it.

"What's the matter?" asked Summer Storm. "Too hot?"

"No," Matt said. "I mean ... uh ... yeah. Sort of." He uttered a feeble laugh.

Summer Storm turned down the heat. Matt squirmed in the chair, feeling around for a slip of paper, but all he found was the smooth vinyl seat. Frantically he ran his hands over all the warm surfaces of the dryer.

"You have to sit still or your Flamingo won't set," Summer Storm warned him.

Matt shoved the dryer off his head and tore off his plastic apron. "I've gotta go."

"But your Flamingo …!"

Matt threw the money for the useless hairdo on the counter and slammed the door behind him.

Laughing, David pointed to Matt's head. "Who's your friend?"

"What do you think?" Matt answered in disgust. "It's a Purple Flamingo."

"Well, you look terrible," David said bluntly. "But at least we can get on with the treasure hunt now, right?"

"Wrong."

"What?"

"There was no clue."

"What?" David said again.

"You heard me. I said there was no clue."

"Did you check …?"

Matt shouted, "I checked everything! Over

69

and over! Do you think I wanted to look like this for nothing?!"

David's shoulders drooped. "I'm sorry. I should never have let you do this."

"There's nothing to be sorry about, David. You said a long time ago this whole thing was fishy, and you were right. We should never have even looked for that clue in the library." Matt yanked the crumpled remains of the library note out of his pocket and tossed them in the garbage. "This so-called treasure hunt is over. If it wasn't for me being such a stupid dork, we never would have gone this far." Matt shoved his hands deep in his pockets and headed across the street.

David followed. "Where are you going?"

Matt tugged at his purple hair. "To get rid of this! Where do you think?!"

8

STORMING INTO THE ice cream store, Matt almost collided with a couple coming out hand in hand. The girl's strawberry-pink ice cream matched her hair. The guy's pistachio-green ice cream matched his.

Matt charged into the men's washroom at the back of the store. He shoved his head under the tap, muttering crossly. As the sink filled with purple water, David sat down on the floor. A minute later, staring up at something, he spoke.

His head still under the tap, Matt snapped, "I can't hear you."

Jumping up, David shouted, "Under the dryer — look!"

Matt turned off the taps. From the underside of the hand dryer, David pulled a piece of paper. When he unfolded it, Matt recognized right away the tight, squeezed-up printing. He recalled the words in the last note. *Where you feel hot air.* "You mean we were supposed to be looking here the whole time? And not in The Purple Flamingo?"

"Yeah," David said. "But something's not right. The clue said something about *colours many* and this place is nothing but grey walls."

"Well, duh!" Matt said. "And how many flavours of ice cream do they sell here?"

David slapped himself in the head. "Of course!"

Matt shook clear water from his once-again-brown hair.

"So, I guess the treasure hunt is still on then, eh?"

Matt grabbed a wad of paper towels and squeezed the water from his hair. "It depends. Let me see that clue you just found. I'm not doing anything stupid like the Purple Flamingo again."

David flattened the paper against the wall.

You've come a long way.
You're almost through.
There's not much more you have to do.
A house on Booth is bigger than the rest.
It has in its yard an old bird's nest.
Don't worry about disturbing the birds,
There aren't any in there, only words.

"Isn't that …?" Matt asked weakly.

David nodded. "Mr. Grubb's place."

"Man!" Matt pounded his fist against the hand dryer. "Haven't we done enough already?"

Matt and David stood staring at the one house on Booth Street that was *much bigger than the rest*. Some of its bricks were chipped or broken. The paint around the eaves and top-floor windows was cracked and peeling. Around the dark, two-storey house grew a tall, prickly hedge. It was the biggest house on the biggest lot on the street.

"So …" David said, "the next clue is in Mr. Grubb's yard."

Suddenly a front window sprang open and clouds of smoke billowed out. Green smoke that seemed to crawl over the windowsill and slither to the floor of the porch. Through the haze, the grey form of Mr. Grubb appeared. With one strong hand, he slammed the window shut.

Without taking his eyes from the window, Matt whispered, "Did you see …?"

David just whimpered in reply.

The boys raced around the corner, but kept their eyes on the house. The front door opened. The old man appeared. He was carrying a large plastic bag that bulged with … something. Matt didn't want to even guess with what. Crouched behind the hedge, through quivering leaves the boys peered. Matt was afraid that the loud thudding of his heart might give away their hiding place in the deadly quiet of the hot morning.

The shrill squeak of the gate broke the silence. It sounded like a scream of pain, and was repeated when Mr. Grubb pulled the gate shut behind him. The large owner of the big, old house shuffled down Booth Street and disappeared into the ravine.

"I don't like this," Matt whispered.

"Are you scared?" David asked.

"Are you?"

David nodded. "But I'm kind of curious, too."

"Well, don't forget," Matt warned, "curiosity killed the dog."

David corrected him. "Curiosity killed the cat."

"Whatever."

The boys crept down the side of Mr. Grubb's yard. Along the back of the property, thick bramble bushes pushed against a dilapidated fence. In the corner of the yard, just beyond the brambles, grew an oddly shaped tree with one dead branch. Sitting on the dead branch were the scraggly remains of a bird nest.

"That's it," said Matt. "The clue in that nest could lead us to the treasure."

Through a quiet lunch, Matt thought about the note in the nest and wondered how many more clues there were going to be. Leaving most of his sandwich on the plate, he mumbled excuses to his mother.

He pedalled alone into the ravine and along the dirt path to his quiet spot by the river. He flipped a stone, ready to count how many times it skipped. But it sank immediately without skipping even once.

Matt sighed. He and David knew the exact whereabouts of the next clue. But they also knew they could not possibly go into Mr. Grubb's yard to get it. So, in spite of all they'd been through, it again looked like the treasure hunt was over.

Unless there was another way of getting that clue.

Matt flung another stone across the water. Three skips.

There had to be a way.

What if they were to climb the stone wall between David's yard and Mr. Grubb's? The nest might be too far into Mr. Grubb's yard for them to reach, but maybe it wasn't. Or — if it was too far — maybe they could use a ladder, and one of them could crawl along the branch to the nest. It would have to be David. He was lighter. Besides, Matt had already done one scary thing at the Purple Flamingo. It was David's turn.

But what if the branch wouldn't take even David's weight? David would go crashing down into Mr. Grubb's yard and be trapped there.

If only there was a way of getting into the yard knowing for sure that Mr. Grubb wouldn't see them. Like, if they knew Mr. Grubb was out and wouldn't be home for a long enough time.

But how would they know that?

Maybe – Matt picked up a flat stone and squeezed it in his fist. What if, when they knew that Mr. Grubb was asleep … That was it! That's how they could get the clue out of the tree!

Matt flipped the stone across the creek and counted. Fourteen skips. Ha! They would find this treasure yet!

Up the bank and through the bushes to the boulder Matt scrambled. He couldn't wait to tell David his idea.

Matt leaned his bike against David's house. Expecting to find David reading in the hammock, he ran into the backyard. The hammock hung empty between the trees. Matt was about to leave, but then he spotted him. On top of the stone wall, near the back corner of his yard! He was on his knees, reaching toward the abandoned nest on the branch of the tree in Mr. Grubb's yard. David was trying to get the next clue! Without him!

9

"HEY!"

When Matt shouted, David lost his balance. He almost toppled into the yard next door, but threw himself down into his own at the last moment.

"What's the big idea?" Matt yelled.

David wiped sweat from his brow. "What do you mean?"

"Going ahead on the treasure hunt without me! That's what!"

"I just thought if we could get the next clue without going right into Mr. Grubb's yard ..."

"*We* were not going for the next clue, David. *You* were. Alone."

David shrugged.

"You were trying to get the treasure without me, weren't you?" accused Matt. "*My treasure!*"

"*Your* treasure?" David folded his arms. "You would never have got this far without me, and you know it!"

"Would, too!"

"Would not! You're a quitter, Matt. Every time things got a bit tough, you quit! I should never have agreed to split the treasure with you."

"It was never yours to split!" Matt yelled. "*I'm* the one who got the first clue — on the postcard, remember?" Clenching his fists against his hips, he glared at David and stepped toward him.

"Sure, I remember," David argued. "But I also remember who helped you get the clue in the library, and I remember who found the clue under the hand dryer, too."

"You didn't even know the clue was there! If I hadn't had the guts to go into The Purple Flamingo to get my hair done, you would never even have been near that dryer!"

"Oh, you had the guts, all right." Marching past the hammock, David grabbed his book and laughed. "And you were just stupid enough to do it, too."

Speechless, Matt stormed out of the yard right behind him.

David mounted his glistening red BMX. "What a stupid waste of *my* money that little escapade was!" he said, and pedalled off toward the ravine.

Matt cursed the chain on his own bike that was once again dangling. After fixing it, he sped to catch up with David. Pulling up alongside him on the ravine path, he said, "Maybe I'm not as smart as you are, but at least I'm not a traitor."

David snarled, "I am not a traitor."

"Then what were you doing up on that wall?"

"The nest was still out of reach."

Matt kept pressing. "But what if you could have reached it? You were going to cut me out, weren't you?"

"If you think I'm a traitor," David sneered,

"then I guess you already have your answer."

Matt pulled out ahead and turned abruptly into David's path.

David swerved to avoid a collision and his front wheel caught the edge of the pavement. The gleaming red bicycle crashed to the ground, pinning David beneath it. He groaned, "I can't move."

Matt rode on into the ravine. "So?" he called back. "You've got a book in your pocket. Why don't you read it?" He left David lying where he'd fallen. But tears stung his eyes as he pedalled on.

Nestled in the sand by his spot on the river, Matt felt wretched. He hadn't wanted to involve David in the search for clues to start with. Why had he ever started to trust him? What if he hadn't caught him up on the wall? What if David had reached the nest before Matt got there? Would he have bothered telling Matt that he'd found the next clue? Why did Matt want so much to believe that David had not intended to cut him out of things?

Matt sighed. David had called him a quitter, and stupid, too. Matt knew he was no brainer. And he *had* wanted to give up, more than once.

Matt thought about the riding he and David had done together since that first day on the bridge. He thought about how they'd shared ice cream cones, and about their adventures tracking down clues. He knew, then, why it mattered if David had been planning to go ahead with the treasure hunt without him. It mattered, because you can only be a traitor to a friend. And that's what David had become, sometime when Matt wasn't looking.

Matt rode back to where he had left David in the ravine, but David was gone. He rode past David's house, but his bike wasn't there. He continued on — around the corner past Mr. Grubb's, through the schoolyard, and on down Stony Road. But there was no sign of David or his bike anywhere.

Matt wandered into the variety store and slouched against the counter. Martha pushed a wisp of hair behind her ear. "Why so sad?" she asked. "It can't be that bad."

Did she always speak in rhyme like that? Was she the person who'd written the clues? At that moment, Matt didn't particularly care. "Martha," he said, "have you ever been really rotten to someone?"

"I made Lisa eat her vegetables when I was babysitting. Rotten like that?"

"No. I mean like to a friend."

"I told Rapture she was ugly once."

"Well, she is, kind of. The way she … you know."

"It was still rotten of me to say so. Just because her style isn't my style. It really hurt her feelings."

"So, what did she do?"

"She accused me of being plain and said I was jealous of how she looked because I couldn't afford to spend a lot on makeup and getting my hair done and all that."

"Did you get mad?"

"I was mad at first. Then I realized I *am* plain,

and that's okay. But sometimes people say things they think will hurt you when they're feeling hurt or insecure."

"So, what did you do?"

"I apologized."

"Even though Rapture *is* kind of ugly?"

"She's not, really. Not once you get to know her."

Matt moved away from the counter. "I guess lots of people aren't what you think at first." The bell on the door of the variety store jingled. Matt looked up. He almost hoped it would be Rapture coming in, so he could look at her and try to see her as not ugly.

"Now remember, Lisa," Mrs. Miffin said, "just look. Don't touch."

"Yook don't touch," shouted Lisa, running up and down the aisles. "Yook don't touch!" She wrapped her pudgy arms around Matt's legs, but he managed to escape.

Through the streets of Pebble Creek, Matt rode and rode. He found David, finally, at the wooden bridge, dangling his feet in the water and reading his book.

Although Matt had looked hard for David, now that he found him his stomach went into knots. He lay his bike down on the ground. "I'm sorry, David. Were you hurt? Before? When? — you know?"

David continued to read.

"David?"

"It depends what you mean. If you're talking about my scraped leg, not really. If you're talking about being called a traitor ..."

"I'm sorry. The way it looked ..."

"You accused me of something before you even knew the facts. Where were you after lunch?"

As Matt tried to remember, David went on. "Your mom said you'd gone riding, but I couldn't find you anywhere."

Matt remembered where he had been. No one would find him there.

David continued. "So I thought I'd just see if

my idea for getting the nest was even possible." He set his book down on the bridge between them. "I figured you'd show up eventually, and you did. But before I could explain, you started in about *your* treasure, and the next thing I know I'm lying on the ground underneath my bike and you're riding away."

Sunlight glinted on the ripples of water below the bridge. Matt said, "You know how you're smarter than me?"

David sighed.

"Well, you are."

"So?"

"Well, after lunch I thought of a way for us to get the clue in the nest, and it wouldn't even be dangerous. Well, hardly at all. So I came racing over to your place to tell you about it. I felt good, because I knew you had kind of kept us going up till now. I thought if I figured out about the clue in the nest ..."

David nodded. "So, you come into my yard, and it looks like I'm about to get the sixth clue without you. So much for your chance to show off your brainy idea."

"Yeah."

"So, you decide I'm a traitor and who knows what else, and cut me off in the path."

"You were really bugging me, David. You were acting just like you do when school's on. You know … all high and mighty, like you think you're better than everyone else."

"That's not what I think." David shook his head. "But when you started in about *your* treasure, I was afraid you were going to cut me out of the hunt."

"I thought *you* were trying to cut *me* out," said Matt.

Sitting on the bridge, the boys were silent for a moment.

David pulled his feet from the water. "So what was your idea? About the clue in the nest? Do you still want to tell me?"

Matt thought about it for only a moment. "Do you have a tent?" he asked.

"No."

"That's okay," Matt said. "I do."

"What does a tent have to do with the note in the nest?"

"Do you think your parents would let us sleep out in your backyard tonight? In my tent?"

"Probably. But ..."

"Listen." Matt said, "Out in the tent, we wait. And when everyone is asleep, including Mr. Grubb ..."

David nodded and smiled. "... under cover of darkness, we go ..."

10

IN MATT'S NYLON tent, the boys waited. A sliver of orange sun disappeared behind the school, and darkness soon closed in.

From the dark bulk of the house next door, no light shone. The blinds on the upstairs windows were down. Behind one of them, the boys guessed, slept Mr. Grubb. Behind the other? They hated to imagine. Without a word, they crawled out of the tent. On silent feet they stole out of David's yard and down his driveway. Matt carried a bottle of cooking oil with him. When he stopped at the sidewalk, David bumped into him.

"Sshh!" Matt warned. But the only sound on the street was the chirping of the crickets in the long grass down by the creek.

A cat on a neighbour's porch watched as the two boys in pyjamas crept along the hedge in front of Mr. Grubb's dark house. Moths fluttered around a streetlight. At the gate, Matt took the lid off the bottle and dribbled oil down each of the rusty hinges. He set the bottle down, lifted the catch on the gate, and slowly pushed it open.

All quiet. Matt made the okay sign with his fingers. He and David stepped beyond the gate.

In one of the front windows, the window of the green smoke, a strange play of light and dark froze Matt in mid-step. Inside the house, had something moved? Or had he seen just the flickering reflection of a streetlight?

What was that — that rustling in the bushes by the porch?

David grabbed the sleeve of Matt's pyjamas and Matt gasped. David whispered, "How did you talk me into this?" Together, into the dreaded yard, the boys followed their eerie shadows.

Creeping through the damp, overgrown grass,

Matt tried hard not to imagine the things that might be crawling in the ivy that clung to the walls of the old house. The back of the house, when they got there, was still in darkness. The blinds were still down. Matt continued on tiptoe toward the crooked tree.

"Do you think we'll be able to reach the nest?" he whispered. "It looks pretty high."

David didn't answer.

"David?" Matt turned.

But David was gone. Where was he? Matt scanned the yard.

Beside a gnarled rose bush stood a shovel. What had David told him about bodies in the garden? Matt strained his eyes in the darkness, but he couldn't see David among the trees and bushes, and he couldn't see him along the stone wall. He couldn't see David anywhere.

Could David have chickened out and gone back to his own yard? Or had he been mysteriously taken into ... that house? Matt shuddered. He didn't know if he should stay there, where trees seemed to be coming to life and reaching out all around him, or if he should escape while he had the chance. Where was David? If only he knew.

Then he saw him. He was standing by Mr. Grubb's back door.

"What ...?" Matt hurried to David's side. He was poking through old paperback books that were stacked up on a TV tray.

"You dweeb! What do you think this is? Some friendly trip to the library?!"

From inside the house came a sudden *zzzt-zzzt* sound, a brilliant flash of blue, and the sound of running water. David dropped his book. Matt hunched against the wall and listened until the sound stopped. Slowly he stood up and peered over the window sill into the kitchen.

In the middle of the room there was an old-fashioned camera on a very tall tripod. Attached to the tripod was a large digital clock. Water was running from the taps into the sink. Tubes ran from the sink to various pots around the room.

More tubes ran out of the room to other parts of the house. When the water reached the top of the sink, the taps shut off. But there was no one there.

Matt and David looked at each other, wide-eyed. Again they heard *zzzt-zzzt*, followed by a brilliant blue flash. Matt pulled David away from the window. "Come on," he whispered. "This house is haunted. Let's go get that clue. Before it's too late."

Cold squooshed between the boys' toes as they crossed the grass. A chill breeze made them shiver in their light pyjamas. From the corner of Mr. Grubb's long yard, the twisted branches of the tree that held the abandoned nest seemed to beckon them closer, daring them to try to get the note that was waiting there.

Matt looked at David. "Just a tree, right?"

"Right."

Beside the tree Matt hunched over so that David, who was the lighter of the two, could climb up on his back.

"Ooogh!" Matt complained, wobbling under

David's weight, "your feet are wet!"

"Wait!" David shouted.

Together, the boys fell in a tangled heap.

"Man, for a lightweight, you're heavy," Matt moaned.

Then he clutched David's arm and squeezed it. "Look."

The blind on an upper window was up. Behind the smeary glass was the grey shape of a very large man. The grey shape turned, leaving the window empty.

"It's Mr. Grubb," David wailed. "He's coming."

"Let's get out of here — quick — before he gets downstairs!"

Tripping over their own and each other's feet, Matt and David scurried toward the gate. They were almost there when they heard deep, bellowing laughter. It sounded like some kind of maniac ghost. Huffing and panting, the boys kept running till they were safely back inside Matt's tent. There they huddled, shivering, deep into their sleeping bags.

"So," Matt said, when the light next door finally went out again, "I guess you didn't get it, eh?"

David crinkled the paper in the dark. "Got your flashlight?"

Matt flicked it on. He shone it on the paper in David's hands. "Hold still," he said.

"You're the one who's shaking," said David.

Matt tried to hold the flashlight steady. David took a deep breath and read:

> You've come very close to my big house old,
> But to come right inside, are you that bold?
> To get the treasure, that's what you must do,
> So into my home I'm inviting you.
> Go down the hall, take the second right,
> And in that room you will see the sight
> You've been searching for all this time.
> But I warn you now — there's another rhyme.

Matt's heart sank. "Mr. Grubb wrote these notes?"

"Looks like it."

Matt pulled his sleeping bag over his head. David clicked off the flashlight.

"I can't believe it was Mr. Grubb," David said. "I was sure it was Martha."

"Well, for once you were wrong." Matt poked his head back out of his sleeping bag. "I was kind of hoping it was a stranger who did them. Like, you know on that channel that shows all the old black-and-white TV shows? Where this guy goes around mysteriously sending people a million dollars? Somebody like that."

"Maybe Mr. Grubb *is* somebody like that."

"I doubt it," Matt muttered.

David folded his arms behind his head and stared up at the roof of the tent. "It was pretty clever of the old creep just the same."

"Mmhm."

"So," David said, "I wonder what the treasure is."

"Who cares? We're not going into that house just because some stupid note says to. Especially not after what we saw tonight."

David said nothing.

Firmly, Matt said, "Right, David?"

"I don't know. We've been over there once already. At night! What could be scarier than that?"

"There's a big difference between sneaking around somebody's yard when they're sleeping, and going right into their house."

"You quit if you want, Matt," David said. "But I've got to know why Mr. Grubb did this. I'm going to go in whether you do or not."

Matt stared at the ceiling of the tent. Wishing he had never seen the mysterious postcard that had lured him into this mess, he pulled his sleeping bag up over his head.

11

PRETENDING TO READ comics on Matt's front porch, Matt and David waited and watched, and watched and waited.

Finally Mr. Grubb emerged from the old house at the end of the street. He shuffled down the steps and down the walk. After opening the gate, he paused. After closing it, he stuck a finger in one ear and then the other. A puzzled look on his sour face, he bent down.

"The oil," said Matt. "I forgot to pick up the bottle of oil on my way out of the yard."

Mr. Grubb shook his head and coughed. It sounded almost like a laugh.

David was right. They couldn't back out now.

Not after coming this far. Or this close. Besides, if David could go on, there was no reason Matt couldn't, too. He scribbled a message on a sheet of paper: *Dear Mom, Gone to Mr G's with David. Matt*

Again only the neighbour's cat watched as the boys approached the house. This time no smoke billowed from windows and there were no flashes of light. The only sound was a *creak-creak* as they climbed the old, wooden stairs.

On the porch, Matt took a deep breath. He opened the screen door and, with David, stepped into the house. The door sprang shut behind them.

In the musty-smelling hall, pictures of Mr. Grubb and of people who must be his ancestors lined the walls. The eyes in the photos followed the boys as they tiptoed down the hall. In a room on their left, big, dark shapes seemed almost to be waiting for them.

David whispered, "It's just furniture."

"Sure," Matt whispered back. "What else would it be?"

Down the quiet, dingy hall they crept.

"What are all these tubes and wires and things for?" David asked.

Matt noticed them for the first time — a twisting mass of red and yellow tubes and wires that snaked along the floor and trailed deeper and deeper into the house. "A trap maybe? Let's go."

But David insisted on following them to see where they led, and Matt followed.

Soon the boys found themselves standing in the kitchen. The tubes and wires crossed the floor to the sink where they attached to an octopus-like contraption. Green tubes stretched from there to various exotic-looking plants around the room. *Zzzt-zzzt!*

Before Matt could remember why the sound was familiar, a flash of blue light filled the kitchen. He turned and noticed a yellow wire that wiggled across the floor to a tripod. Attached to the tripod was a camera and a clock. A photograph of one of the strange plants slid from the camera into a tray beneath it. The time was printed in the bottom corner.

All by itself, it seemed, the camera rotated. When the clock read 2:02, there was another *zzzt-zzzt* and another flash of blue. Moments later, another photo slid into the tray.

"This is weird," Matt said.

"Mr. Grubb must have programmed a computer — somewhere — to water his plants and take pictures of them," said David.

"But why?"

"For fun?"

"Oh, yeah, that's real fun."

"Let's see what this is," said David, following another trail of wires. They disappeared under a closed door.

Matt said, "We better not go in."

"Why not?" David put his hand on the knob.

"Well ... because ... we weren't invited in there." Matt didn't want to admit he was scared silly. "Get the note. Which room does it say the treasure's in?"

David said, "It's probably locked anyway."

But when he turned the knob, the door opened.

"Phew!" David reeled back, closing the door again quickly. Covering his nose, he said, "He must have dead bodies in there."

"No, that smell is like the stuff they use at The Purple Flamingo," Matt said. "Only stronger." And he made himself peer into the room.

Glass bottles and beakers and metal pots perched on tables, and more tubing twisted around them. In some containers, brilliantly coloured liquids glistened and shone.

"What does he *do* in here?"

"Remember the green smoke?" asked David.

Matt croaked, "How could I forget?" A single bubble burbled through a beaker of red liquid and popped. Matt quickly pulled the door shut.

Along the hall, more wires of various colours and thicknesses twisted. They disappeared up a shadowy staircase.

"No way," insisted Matt. "Let's just hurry up and find what we came here for. Which room did the clue say it's in?"

David reread the note. "The second room on the right. That's counting from the front door."

"This one, then." Matt whispered, but wasn't sure why. He and David exchanged brave smiles and turned the corner into the room.

It was a small room almost completely taken up with an old rolltop desk. On the desk sat a computer, and around it were several chairs. Matt said, "I don't get it."

"Well, I guess compared to the *old* desk, the computer is *new*," David said. But clearly he was puzzled, too — and disappointed. So, the weird old man with the fancy plants and camera also had a computer. So, it happened to have a huge, cool, flat-screen, thin monitor. This was this supposed to be the *treasure*?

A large sticky note was stuck to the edge of the monitor. David pulled it off.

"You want to read it?" Matt said. His heart wasn't in it. David read:

The end of any treasure hunt
calls for celebration.
So now's the time I offer you
a special invitation
To play computer games with me
and Betsy any day
That you have asked your mothers
and they've said, it's okay.
I knew you'd come here first
with me gone, somehow,
But on the desktop, double-click
"Treasure Hunt" now.

"Yeah, right," Matt mumbled. "Let's go."

"What? After all we've done to get here, you don't even want to check it out?"

"Playing some dumb computer game with some old guy is no *treasure*! And who's Betsy anyway? The Wicked Witch of the West?"

David shrugged. "Let's just see what happens."

Before Matt could stop him, David reached for the mouse and double-clicked the *Treasure*

Hunt icon. Right away the huge, flat-screen monitor immediately filled with exploding colours, and a husky female voice began to sing. "I'm Betsy and I know some games you know for sure, like Bookworm and Baseball, and so many more …"

"I know that voice!" Matt said. "That's Rapture! What's she …?"

"Shh! Listen!"

The song finished, "But the best things are for the Computer Club, That you can join … with Mr. Archibald Grubb."

"Those two weirdos …?"

"Maybe you're right, Matt. We better get out of here. Now. While we still can."

Matt slapped David on the back. "Finally we agree. Let's go!"

But at the doorway of the room they were stopped cold by the towering bulk of Mr. Archibald Grubb.

12

THE OLD MAN'S gravelly voice rumbled, "I declare this the first official meeting of the newly formed Computer Club ..."

Matt felt faint. Spinning through his head were images of the old man and his computer, of twisting wires, and of Rapture's hands rubbing shampoo into his head. On Mr. Grubb's computer, her voice began to sing again. "I'm Betsy and I know some ..." Matt couldn't help but notice how much better the sound quality was than the sound on any stereo he'd ever heard.

Mr. Grubb reached out his long arm and the voice was silenced. Matt was thinking about sound quality when his very life might be in danger!

The old man mumbled quietly, "... consisting of Matt Randall, David Varvarikos, and Archibald Grubb. That's me."

Matt felt himself nodding. David was nodding, too.

"Sit down, Matt," the grey voice growled. "You're the baseball star, aren't you?"

Matt sat. Mr. Grubb stabbed the keyboard with his long, bony fingers. From speakers near the ceiling came the sounds of a cheering crowd. The screen filled with the sight of a stadium packed with fans. Matt could have sworn he was in a real stadium. David slowly moved backward toward the door.

"You sit, too," ordered Mr. Grubb, and David sat.

"Hot dogs! Get your hot dogs!"

Matt spun around to find the hot dog vendor. Not only was the voice incredibly realistic, Matt was sure he could smell mustard, too. But the voice was, of course, coming from the computer, and the only hot dogs were virtual ones.

When Matt looked back to the screen, players were jogging onto an emerald-green baseball diamond. A team in red uniforms took the infield, a team in blue the outfield. The graphics were so clear and so detailed, Matt could almost see the stitching around each player's number.

Mr. Grubb handed Matt a game pad.

"What do I do?" He had played computer baseball before, of course. But comparing the versions he had played before to the one on Mr. Grubb's computer was like comparing Bugs Bunny and *The Lord of the Rings*. Who ever would have thought an old guy like Mr. Grubb would have not only a really cool computer, but all the best software, too?

Mr. Grubb showed Matt where to place his thumbs and fingers on the game pad's controls. *Something old with something new. Big parts and little parts.* No one could have guessed it, but it made perfect sense.

Following Mr. Grubb's directions, Matt soon got his player to hit a home run. Beads of sweat formed on his brow, and dust was kicked up by his feet. Matt almost laughed out loud, the game was that fantastic.

And according to Mr. Grubb, he could play it anytime he wanted. No more fighting for a turn on the video games at the ice cream store. They weren't half as good as this anyway. No more waiting at the library to get on the Internet either. This was great!

"Sit tight, David," said Mr. Grubb. "There's a game on here you'll like, too."

Noticing David perched on the edge of a chair, Matt realized he had forgotten all about trying to get away. He had let the baseball game fool him into feeling safe! How could he?! Mr. Grubb was the guy everyone said had bodies buried in his garden. So what if this computer stuff was the best Matt had ever seen?

He shook his head. "I've got to go," he said. "My ..." But before he could finish, something happened on the screen. It happened so quickly he missed seeing it properly. But suddenly, from underneath the computer, a small drawer shot out.

It was full of eyeballs.

Choking back a scream, Matt looked from the eyeballs to the old man and back to the eyeballs again.

They were — oh, man! — gummi eyeballs, his favourite kind of candy. Candy!

A deep, bellowing laugh filled the room. Matt stared at the huge man beside him, too large for his frayed, grey clothes. Mr. Grubb threw back his head as he laughed, and his whole body shook. His jowly face grew redder and redder.

This was their chance to get away — when the old man was distracted. Matt glanced at David and nodded toward the door. The boys started to ease themselves out of their seats.

As suddenly as he had begun laughing, Mr. Grubb stopped. Wiping tears from the wrinkled corners of his eyes, he said "I can't remember the last time I laughed like that. Thank you, Matt."

Thank you? For making him laugh? Matt shrugged.

"Now," growled Mr. Grubb. "Who likes lemonade?"

"I do," answered David. Matt rolled his eyes.

"Good," said Mr. Grubb. "I'll make some." He lifted his big body from the chair and shuffled toward the kitchen at the back of the house.

"What is with '*I do*'?" Matt snapped. "We've got to get out of here."

"Come on, Matt. It would be rude to leave when he's getting us a drink."

"You're worried about being rude? What if the guy's mixing up a batch of poison?"

Mr. Grubb called from the kitchen. "You boys coming?"

Reluctantly, still feeling on his guard, Matt followed David to the kitchen.

The camera and tripod were leaning against the corner. Mr. Grubb was impatiently yanking plastic tubing from the sink and trying to cram it into a cupboard. "Never works," he mumbled. "Stupid thing. Sit down. Now ... what ...?" Mr. Grubb closed his eyes and held his head in his hands. "Lemons!" he exclaimed.

He gathered lemons from the refrigerator and set them on the table. Matt and David watched carefully as the old man cut the lemons in half.

"Does Betsy ever help you make lemonade?" asked David.

"Ho, ho, oh, no," said Mr. Grubb. "Some things must be done the natural way." He squeezed the lemon juice into a glass pitcher. "I did try once to get Betsy to make lemonade. Hooked her up to a food processor. But the pair of them ..." Mr. Grubb chuckled. "I couldn't get them to quit blowing fuses."

At the tap Mr. Grubb added water to the pitcher of lemon juice. From a clay pot he swirled golden honey into the mixture. "Newfangled technology may be good for some things," he said. He waved a long-handled wooden spoon in the direction of the computer room. "But some things are best left to old-fashioned ways." He plopped the spoon into the pitcher and began to stir. Ice cubes clinked against the glass.

"But why do you make lemonade the hard way?" Matt asked. "My mom just opens a package of powder and dumps it in a glass of water."

"Yes, I'm not surprised. Your mother and I have had spirited debates about pie fillings, too."

Mr. Grubb slurped a mouthful of lemonade from the spoon. He filled another spoon and held it out to Matt. "Here. Taste."

Matt sipped the tart liquid from the spoon. "Mmm!"

"Ever taste lemonade like that before?"

Matt licked his lips. "No way. That's great."

"Here, David, you taste."

"Mmmm," David agreed.

Mr. Grubb put ice cubes in three glasses, poured in the lemonade and shook his head. "Dumps a package of powder into a glass of water and calls it lemonade. Tsk, tsk. I bet she pulls a Captain Seafood package out of the freezer and calls it fish, too, does she?"

Matt shrugged and nodded.

"You know, when I was a boy, we used to catch

fish right out of Pebble Creek and cook them up for supper."

Matt and David sipped their lemonade while Mr. Grubb talked on.

"I remember one place I loved to fish. It was beautiful there, the way the sandy bank curved around. I'd just lean back with my line dangling in the water, and look up into the trees. It was kind of a tricky place to get at, so nobody knew about it but me. Other kids started along the path sometimes, but they always turned around when they came to the boulder. Looked like a dead end. I wonder if that old boulder's still there …"

"Yeah, it is." Matt could hardly believe it. *His* secret place had been Mr. Grubb's secret place? All those years ago? "I found that spot, too," Matt said. "It's been my secret place for a long time."

Matt looked at the old man's face more closely. In his grey eyes there was a sparkle, and behind the bushy eyebrows and saggy cheeks, Matt thought he could almost see the face of a young boy. "At least, I thought it was."

Until now, Matt had never thought of sharing his special spot with anyone. It seemed to be a place for him alone. But maybe it was a place to share, too — with a friend.

Matt gulped down the rest of his lemonade. "Come on, David. You've got to see this place."

David jumped up eagerly and started to follow Matt out of the room. At the doorway, both boys stopped. Behind them, Mr. Grubb was busily clearing up the lemonade glasses.

Matt walked back over to him and held out his hand. "Thanks a lot, Mr. Grubb. For everything. We'll be back tomorrow, okay?"

Mr. Grubb solemnly shook Matt's hand. "I would like that, my friend," he said, smiling. "I'd like that … very much."

Read more of Matt's adventures in Pebble Creek!

The Great Bike Race

Matt leaned over his handlebars, ready for the Go. Sweat trickled down the side of his face. He reached up to wipe it away. Bang!

Can Matt win the town's bike race? He thinks so. Not only is he fast, but he really needs the first prize- an awesome new mountain bike-to replace his old clunker. But Matt's pals all think they can win, too. And practising for the race seems to bring out the worst in everyone. Pretty soon the competitors are barely speaking. Can Matt stay friends with the others after the race is over? If he loses, will he want to?

The Great Bike Race is the second book in Kathy Stinson's trilogy of adventure stories set in Pebble Creek. Enjoy it with *Seven Clues* and *One More Clue*- or each story on its own!

ISBN10 1-55028-888-1
ISBN13 978-1-55028-888-9 $8.95

Read more of Matt's adventures in Pebble Creek!

One More Clue

While cleaning his neighbour's attic, Matt uncovers two mysterious items: a magician's costume and a poem written on a dusty, yellowed piece of paper.

There's something you should look for
Which I hope that you will treasure
Searching for it by yourself
Is important beyond measure

Could it be an ancient clue for some long-ago treasure hunt? With the help of his friends, Matt sets out to discover the history of this decades-old mystery—and possibly a treasure!

One More Clue is the third book in Kathy Stinson's trilogy of adventure stories set in Pebble Creek. Enjoy it with *Seven Clues* and *The Great Bike Race*-or each story on its own!

ISBN10 1-55028-890-3
ISBN13 978-1 55028-890-2 $8.95